Anne Fine

A Sudden Glow of Gold

Illustrated by David Higham

mammoth

First published in Great Britain 1991
by Piccadilly Press Ltd
Published 1992 by Mammoth
an imprint of Egmont Children's Books Limited,
a division of Egmont Holding Limited,
239 Kensington High Street, London W8 6SA

This edition first published in 2000
for The Book People Ltd,
Hall Wood Avenue, Haydock, St Helens WA11 9UL

ISBN 0 7497 0256 7

10 9 8 7 6 5 4 3 2 1

A CIP catalogue record for this title
is available from the British Library

Printed in Great Britain
by Cox & Wyman Ltd, Reading, Berkshire

CHAPTER ONE

Toby slammed the door shut. He would have stamped his foot if there had been anywhere to stamp it. But that was part of the problem. His bedroom floor was knee-deep in clutter. Simply to get to the bed, he practically had to *wade* through games, models, books, and hundreds of other bits and pieces.

And he'd been told to clear the whole lot up.

"No more excuses!" said Mum. "I don't even want to see your face again, unless you're carrying some of that stuff out of your room."

She meant it, too. Toby could tell.

He picked his way across the room to the safety of his bed. It took real skill to know where to put down a foot and not squash something, or snap something else. This wasn't simple mess, like Sophie Hunter's bedroom. Her room was a pit. Disgusting! Crisp packets, toffee wrappers, dirty socks – and *worse*. Toby didn't even want to think about Sophie Hunter's bedroom.

No, Toby's was different. Everything jammed in his cupboards or on his shelves, or spread out on his floor, was something he'd wanted. Something he'd found or bought or swapped. Something he'd brought home proudly and been glad to have. There was no rubbish in here. And that was why he'd been sent to clear it out by himself. Mum had offered several times before.

"I'll do it for you happily," she'd said. "But I must be allowed to throw some things out."

Throw some things out? No way! Toby needed absolutely everything. Well, maybe *needed* wasn't the right word.

Wanted.

He'd wanted everything. Rolling onto his stomach across the duvet, he took a long hard look around the room. Catching sight of one or two things, it was difficult to remember why he'd wanted them so much. That Rubik cube, for

2

example. Nobody played with them any more. But any craze can come back. You never know . . .

He'd really prefer to keep it, just in case.

How about the Beanos? Surely they could go.

But he might get ill one day, and need something good to read.

What about the games? He'd grown out of most of them, or played them so often he felt he'd never want to play them again.

But he might not be so fed up with them in a few weeks.

The snorkel? No. He might find the ping-pong ball, and manage to get it back inside the tube. The cardboard skeleton? No. Henry had hung from the curtain rail so long he was practically a friend. Surely the plastic vampire's teeth could go?

Oh no they couldn't. It was nearly Hallowe'en.

It was no good. Toby despaired. Everything he'd owned since he was practically a baby was somewhere in this room. His belongings all but flowed up the walls, but there wasn't a single thing that he felt like shoving in a bag and carrying out to the bin, or stacking in a box and taking down to the charity shop.

It was beginning to look as if Toby's mum would never see her dear son's face again.

Toby wriggled to the edge of the bed, and leaned over. Perhaps there was something hidden underneath that he could toss to the winds. The sled? Certainly not. He used that. The wellies? No, they still fitted. Mum would fly out of her cage if he threw those away. And he couldn't throw out his foreign coins or his swimming goggles or his dress-ups. He wore the bat cloak every Hallowe'en, and he needed the baggy

4

trousers to dress up as a pirate whenever his school had a Fun Day.

Wait a minute! What was this, down at the bottom of the box? Of course. It was the rusty old lamp Sophie gave him last year, in case he decided he wanted to be Aladdin for a change. But Toby much preferred pirates. So he could carry the lamp round next door and give it back to Sophie. At least then his mum would get the chance to remember what he looked like!

Toby reached under the bed, and drew the old lamp out into the light. Funny. He hadn't noticed before it had such delicate tracery around the handle and up the little spout. And it was heavier than he remembered. Perhaps it was made of real brass.

Toby gave it a rub.

At first, nothing happened. The dingy metal looked just as dull and rusty as before.

Toby rubbed harder.

"Abracadabra!" he muttered to himself, without thinking. "Abracadabra!" He was so taken up with his rubbing that he didn't notice a long golden fingernail creeping silently over his shoulder.

"Abracadabra!" crooned Toby. "Abracadabra!"

A sudden glow of gold was filling the room. The air warmed, wafting the scent of flowers over his head, and there was a ripple of birdsong.

He still didn't notice. He just kept on rubbing.

"Abracadabra!" he sang merrily. "Abracadabra!"

The long golden fingernail poked Toby hard.

Dropping the lamp in fright, Toby spun round.

A genie, clothed in gold, was standing there watching him through narrowed eyes. The finger that had poked Toby's shoulder was still stretched out threateningly towards him. The golden nail glittered and the genie's eyes flashed.

"Stones of the desert have sharper ears than my master!"

Now, even through his terror, Toby heard the

birdsong and smelled the warm scents, and noticed the golden glow flooding his bedroom.

He couldn't speak. He was too astonished. And far too scared to think of anything to say.

It didn't matter. The genie obviously had a lot to get off his golden chest.

"Any fool knows that it is easier to build two palaces than keep one tidy. But never in all my thousand years have I endured a resting place so like the lair of a jackal."

Toby couldn't help it. The words popped out.

"But you came from Sophie Hunter's room! That's far worse!"

The genie's lip curled at the memory, and just for a moment a picture swam into Toby's mind of this genie standing in Sophie's room amongst all the crumpled chocolate wrappers, the mugs of cold tea with fungus growing on the top – and *worse*. It was a strange vision, because everything about this genie looked so golden and perfect, from the coiled gold turban on his head to the curving gold slippers on his feet. And had he dipped his fingernails in gold, or was he really so magical that parts of him were not even flesh and blood, but made of the most precious metal? This genie looked so polished, so glisten-

8

ing, you'd think he'd be grateful to be safely away from the horrors of Sophie Hunter's bedroom.

But he sounded bad-tempered enough when he spoke.

"It's my opinion that I have fled from the rain, and sat down again under the waterspout."

It was a pity this was a subject on which Toby spent so much time arguing with his mother. As far back as he could remember, she had been comparing his bedroom with Sophie's. "You're really as messy as she is," Mum always said. "Her room may *look* a lot worse, but at least she sometimes flings a few things out. You never do." So now, with the genie starting in on him as well, Toby couldn't help trying to defend himself.

"It's all *clean*," he insisted. "And a lot of it is tidy. It's just that, over the years, I have collected quite a bit of stuff, and there isn't really room for it."

The genie looked scornful.

"The wise man takes care to raise his roof-beams *before* he brings home his camel."

Toby went red. All day, it seemed, he had been under attack about the state of his bedroom. He'd had enough.

"If you think it's such a big mess, you could always go back in your lamp."

Oh, no! What had he *said*? What had he *done*? The genie's eyes flashed sparks of golden fire.

"Beware, boy!" he hissed. "The blessings of an angry genie can fall as curses on his master's head!"

Toby turned his face away. He found it hard to think with those extraordinary golden eyes boring into him. Why had things gone so wrong so quickly? It couldn't be all Toby's fault. The genie was in a bad mood from the start. If all he wanted was to turn Toby's wishes into curses, why had he bothered to come out of the lamp?

Well, he probably had no choice about that. After all, Toby had rubbed it and said "Abracadabra!" And it couldn't be much of a life, spending most of your time trapped in a lamp, and the rest of it granting people's wishes. Toby would be bad-tempered, too, if he was stuck with that job. In fact, he'd hate every minute. He hated being told what to do. Look at this morning. Toby had argued with Mum for hours before she finally ordered him off to his bedroom. And even then he'd slammed the door.

No. Being a genie must be one of the world's worst jobs. Maybe Toby could help, now he was the master of the lamp.

He turned back to face the genie.

"Is there anything that I could wish for you?"

The genie stared.

"Well, twirl my turban!" he said softly between his teeth. "How the world changes as it spins!

You sit like a sultan with all your possessions around you; but when it comes to wishes, you are as different from Hasan's first master as is the generous dove from the greedy magpie!"

Toby tucked his legs more comfortably beneath him on the bed. Suddenly he felt a whole lot safer.

"Tell me about him," he said.

CHAPTER TWO

"My first master –" began the genie. Then he glanced round Toby's small cluttered bedroom with impatience.

"By the fat moon in the sky!" he cried. "Why should I labour to tell you an old tale when, in a flash, I could sweep you away and show you?"

Toby was thrilled.

"Sweep me away? What? On a magic carpet?"

The genie plucked at the duvet, making a scornful face. Then he upturned his palms, and drew his brittle gold fingernails slowly across its cover.

As Toby watched, the duvet grew thinner and

13

shrank to half its size. Patterns appeared on it – the kind of ancient patterns Toby had seen on oriental rugs. Under his legs, the duvet felt different now, more like a soft worn carpet than fluffy bedding. It gave off a musty smell of age. And just as Toby was about to change his mind and beg the genie to stop, there was a sudden glow of gold, a blinding *flash*! and all Toby could feel was wind in his hair, and the carpet rippling beneath him.

He screwed his eyes shut in terror.

Behind him, the genie shouted a warning into the wind:

"Don't look down!"

The golden fingernails slid round Toby's waist. Toby felt safe again. He did try not to look. But it was such a chance, such an extraordinary chance. How could you fly on a magic carpet and not want to see it all?

He opened his eyes.

Above him – blue, blue sky. Around him – the thin wisps of drifting cloud. Beneath him –

"Where on earth is that?"

"It is Arabia."

It was so beautiful. From up so high, the desert was a sea of sand, stretching for ever and

14

ever. Here was a tiny island of palm trees. Miles away, almost out of sight, was another. And moving across the dunes between the two, like ships over waves, Toby saw a long line of camels. Oh, he was lucky to be high up here, winging his effortless way through the cool sky. Down there, the desert burned.

"They have so far to go!"

The genie shrugged.

"The camel is a marvellous beast. She can travel between watersprings for five days in summer and twenty-five in winter. She gives milk to drink. Her dung is fuel for cooking. And when her time is done, her sad owner cheers himself by eating her flesh and making a tent from her skin."

Toby was glad that Hasan couldn't see the look on his face.

"Doesn't seem much of a reward," he said. "For struggling over the desert with all someone's stuff on your back."

"Struggling!" the genie scoffed. "These people know a bird can only roost on one branch. They travel light. A tent, a rug, a sheepskin and a coffee pot! Why, when the Prophet Mohammed himself died, he left behind him only a shirt, a turban and an old patched robe, a waterskin and a palm-leaf mattress."

"Is that *all*? From a whole *life*?"

Behind him, Hasan snorted.

"If every person on earth had as many possessions as you, the world would soon crack from the strain! You will soon find the richest people in this world are not those who have the most things, but those who have the fewest wants.

16

Save your pity for your poor servant Hasan, who would trade all of his golden fingernails for one dish of cooling sherbet!"

Toby was delighted.

"Can I wish for you? *Please*?"

He couldn't see Hasan's face, but he did hear his sudden catch of breath. The genie held him more tightly.

"Is this your first command?"

"My very first!"

The genie's voice was strangely hoarse.

"So be it."

17

A sudden glow of gold warmed Toby's chest and chin. In Hasan's hand there was a sparkling dish of sherbet. One hand still held Toby firmly round the waist as the hand with the sherbet disappeared, and from behind came the tempting sound of Hasan's steady sucking.

The sherbet had looked delicious, and Toby was thirsty too. He was about to ask if he could wish for another, for himself, when suddenly he saw sweeping closer, miles beneath, a palace with glorious towers and gleaming walls.

The carpet flew nearer and nearer. Tiles of blue, green and gold glittered like jewels in the sunlight. The rooftops shone.

"It's beautiful!"

"In its day," said Hasan, "it was the most glorious palace in the world. Mind you, I show it to you at its very best. For many years now it has been nothing but rubble in the sand, and an old memory."

And not a happy one, either, thought Toby, from the tone of Hasan's voice. But, then again, he always sounded a little bit angry and bitter, as if even the golden glory of his dress and nails could not make up for some emptiness inside him. Toby was just wondering what could have happened to make Hasan this way, when suddenly the carpet swooped – down, down – towards the palace so fast that Toby was sure they would smash into its walls. He shut his eyes. But at the very last moment the carpet must have swirled round upon itself, because the next thing he felt was hot sand against his shoulder. The carpet had tumbled the two of them gently off outside the gates.

Toby picked himself up, and brushed off the burning grains of sand. Then he glanced up. The palace towered above them.

"Look at the rooftops! Are they solid gold?"

The genie's eyes followed his. Toby thought

19

he'd be thrilled to see again a place so beautiful, with all its glittering mosaics, its pillars of veined marble, its golden roofs.

But Hasan's face blackened with an old remembered rage.

"Better," he said darkly, "to have a handful of dry dates and be happy than own the Gate of Peacocks and be kicked in the eye by a broody camel."

Toby shrugged. What could he say or do? For

although Hasan had real golden fingernails, and magic at their tips, he was the moodiest creature.

Toby turned away, and peered through the gates into a leafy courtyard.

"Can we go in?"

Hasan rolled up the carpet and tucked it under his arm. Together they walked in. For just a second, Toby felt he'd been here before. But then he realised what was familiar was the sweet flowery scents Hasan brought with him when he first appeared, and the ripple of birdsong.

Hasan sat on the edge of a stone pool, and looked around sadly. Then he spread out his hands. His golden fingernails glittered in the harsh sunlight.

"This is where my story begins. Once, I was happy here . . ."

CHAPTER THREE

"Once," said Hasan, "I was happy here. I came to the palace gates as a young man, hungry and dusty. But I was quick-witted and honest. And since I was from a poor family, I knew the meaning of hard work. I could count coins faster than a hawk can drop, and so the old sultan put me in his treasury, and there I stayed until the day he died."

"And then?"

The first real smile crossed Hasan's face.

"And then the new sultan made me grand vizier."

"Grand vizier!" Toby was astonished. "But

surely that's the most important job!"

"It is indeed. I was chosen for my skills in the treasury. Under my hand, sacks of gold overflowed, and coffers bulged, and for the first time in a hundred years the counting house was as busy as an ant-heap."

"You must have been very proud."

"Proud and happy."

Hasan fell silent. Toby twisted a leaf off the branch of an orange tree behind them. He sat

quietly beside Hasan on the stone ledge of the pool, shredding the leaf to its spine. It was hard to imagine Hasan being happy. He was so – difficult to find a word for it. Hard? No, not *hard*, exactly, because Toby had the feeling there might be quite a warm-blooded person behind those harsh golden stares and sharp flashes of temper. No, it was more as if what softness there was in Hasan was trapped under his golden surface, like water rippling under a crust of ice. But he had been happy here . . .

"Things must have been very different."

"Different!" Hasan's voice was bitter. "The smiles shone from my face. I loved to hear the echo of my own footsteps ringing against the palace walls. I loved to hear the coins in my counting house, tinkling all day like the water from a fountain. But most of all I loved the new young sultan, and I blessed him each morning for giving me my chance to rise in the world – on one condition . . ."

"On one condition? What was that?"

"That I never dare to give him a word of advice about anything in the world that could neither be bought nor sold."

"But almost anything can be bought or sold."

Hasan nodded.

"And I could give advice on almost anything. I could tell him what to do with his coins and his riches. I could warn him, 'Sell that slave,' or urge him, 'Buy this one.' I could advise him about carpets and robes, horses and land, feasts and jewels. I had great power and influence. But

I would lose it all the day I dared to give a word of advice about anything in the land that could neither be bought nor sold."

"I wouldn't have risked it," said Toby after a moment's thought. "Not with a kingdom to run. It would be far too dangerous. You couldn't advise him about any of the really important things, like friends – if they could be trusted. Or war – whether to start one or stop one. Or – "

Hasan's golden eyes flashed.

"You have more wits than I, boy! I never dreamed that trouble would grow underfoot. The only worry I had was whether sacks could be sewn as fast as coins rushed in to fill them. Until the sultan fell in love . . ."

"Love!"

Toby hadn't even thought of that one. You certainly couldn't buy or sell love.

"Her name was Zubaida," said Hasan. "We called her Little Butterpat."

"Why? Was she plump?"

The genie sighed with the pleasure of the memory.

"Oh, she was better than plump! She was as round as the full moon. Once, in the counting house, I put three bulging sacks of gold onto one pan of the scales, and the sultan lifted Little Butterpat onto the other. And her pan floated down."

"It sounds to me as if she was a little bit heavier than plump."

"Yes," cried Hasan. "Why hide the truth about her beauty? Zubaida was not plump. No! She was gloriously, gloriously tubby!"

Toby couldn't help grinning.

"It also sounds to me," he said, "as if you wouldn't have given the sultan very good advice about love in any case. It sounds as if you were a

bit soft on her yourself."

Almost before the words were out of Toby's mouth, the genie's metallic eyes were glittering.

"Be quite clear, little master, I was not 'a bit soft' on Little Butterpat. I kissed the stones on which her silver slippers trod! I sent slaves to sprinkle rosewater wherever she might walk! I sent for the finest songbirds and hung their cages underneath her windows! And each time I went past a butterpat stall in the market-place, I all but fainted with joy!"

Toby took very great care to keep his face straight, and Hasan explained gravely:

"My happiness hung on hers, you see. If Little Butterpat was happy, then so was I."

"And was she?"

"Oh, she was happy as a lark. So was the sultan. Each morning, when he woke, he said to her: 'Bite my finger, beloved, so I may know if this happiness I feel is a dream!' "

"And did she?"

"Did she what?"

"Bite his finger each morning."

The genie stared, then asked irritably:

"Boy! Have you never *loved*?"

Toby gave it a moment's reflection. He'd had a

bit of a crush on Miss Adulewebe for a while, till she told him off twice in a row for doing sloppy work. And Mum often joked about the way he chased Sophie Hunter round the nursery playground, trying to kiss her. But he was only four then.

He was a lot older now. And he certainly wouldn't fancy having his finger bitten every morning.

"No, never," he said firmly. "I've never been in love."

"Then you won't understand," declared Hasan. "You won't know the joy of standing in a courtyard at night watching the one you worship

29

counting the stars! Hearing her guess the words that the songbird you gave her is singing! Listening to her tell her fortune in the dregs of her sherbet!"

Oh, really! thought Toby. Op, plop. Pass the mop! But just at that moment a golden tear began to roll down Hasan's cheek.

"Oh!" he wailed. "I was so happy, here at the fountain beside my master and his beloved, listening to the nightingale!"

In silence Toby waited for the tear to fall with a splash on the hot stones between Hasan's slippers. But:

Ping!

He couldn't have imagined it! The tear was actually rolling away!

"Is that tear made of *real gold*?"

Hasan looked wretched.

"Permit me to weep you a bucketful," he offered.

Toby was horrified.

"No. Please don't! No."

Hasan looked more than ready. On each lower lid, tiny gold tears were welling.

Toby was desperate to distract him.

"I wish – " he cried. (For surely, if Hasan had

work to do, he wouldn't have time to cry.)

"I wish – "

The twin tears trembled. Hasan looked so miserable that Toby could only think of one thing to wish.

"I wish you could be with the sultan and Zubaida again, hearing the nightingale's best song!"

There it was a second time – that little catch of breath. The genie gripped Toby by the elbows

and looked half-mad with hope.

"Is it your second wish?"

For just a moment, Toby hesitated. After all, he didn't know how many wishes he was going to get. It might be only three. He'd already used one up getting Hasan that sherbet. Now he was about to spend another trying to cheer him up.

But what else could he do?

"Yes, it's my second wish."

There was a sudden glow of gold. A brilliant *flash*! And before he knew what had hit him, or how, poor Toby was tumbling – back, back, back, backwards through the hot and scented air, into the water of the pool.

CHAPTER FOUR

Oh, bliss! Oh, heaven! Oh, perfect joy! He hadn't
realised quite how hot he was, till he fell into the
water. It filled his ears, blotting out everything
but tendrils of weed and the spangles of sunlight
above him. There was no room to swim. The pool
was little more than a stone tank, not very much
deeper than a bath. But Toby could stretch himself out – now floating – now letting himself sink
– now using a fingertip to push himself up again.
His hair fanned around his face like more dark
weed. He was perfectly, perfectly happy.

And so, it seemed, was Hasan. Each time Toby
floated up to break the surface and take a lungful

33

of air, he could hear the song of a bird, and snatches of happy chatter. But Toby wouldn't look. What was the point of giving Hasan his wish, and then spoiling it by being nosy? He'd love to peep at Little Butterpat and the sultan. But Hasan wasn't daft. Toby hadn't fetched up underwater by accident. Hasan had tipped him in. It

must be for a reason. Perhaps the moment Toby lifted his head clear of the water to take a look at Hasan's friends, the nightingale would stop singing and the two of them would vanish.

Give him time. Give him time . . .

Did minutes pass? Or hours? Toby lost track. When the gold fingernail dipped in to prod him, all Toby knew was that he'd been left to wallow in the cool water of the stone tank the perfect length of time. No more, no less.

Hasan pulled him out, then stepped back as puddles of water spread from Toby's shoes, threatening his own golden slippers.

"How was the water, little master?"

Toby shook his fringe like a dog, splattering drops all round.

"Perfect," he said. "How did the wish go?"

The genie did try to answer. But Toby could see he couldn't find the words. After a moment he gave up the struggle and, slipping an arm around Toby, said to him instead:

"A walk around the palace, while you dry!"

Together they strolled through the courtyard. First Hasan pushed open the door to the counting house.

"No need to step inside. You can see all you

need from here."

But Toby was curious. After all, this was where Hasan had spent years of his life. Before the genie could stop him, he'd slipped through the door, and taken a good look around. The tables were heaped high with coins, as if Hasan had left off counting only yesterday. Great piles of sacks blocked most of the tiny windows. But in the corner Toby suddenly saw two strange golden statues, lit by a dusty shaft of light. They were taller than Toby, and dressed in the finest robes. Could they be statues of the sultan and Zubaida?

The woman was certainly – what was it? – as round as the full moon. But the man was staring at the woman in shock, and the woman was pointing in anger. That couldn't be right. The sultan and Little Butterpat were supposed to be happy as a dream.

"Who are – "

But Hasan had stepped in after him, and gripping Toby firmly by the arm, hurried him out again.

"Come. There is much more to see."

Much, much more. Toby never forgot the way his eyes were dazzled as the genie led him through one glittering chamber after another, each stuffed with more treasures than the last. At first Toby ran everywhere, trying to touch everything he saw. Later he walked more slowly, and only bothered to stretch out a hand to pat the ivory saddle of this rocking horse, or lift a jewelled piece from that chess board. And by the time Hasan had led him all the way round the palace and back to where they began, Toby was stifling a yawn.

"So much *stuff*!"

Behind, through the door of the counting house, Toby heard a little sob. But in there stood only the two golden statues. He would have thought that he'd imagined it, but when he turned back he was just in time to see the look of pain crossing Hasan's face.

"Did you hear someone sobbing?"

Hasan's face went stony.

"No one is there, little master."

"But I heard someone sobbing. So did you."

Stubbornly, Hasan repeated:

"No one is there. It is the echo of a memory."

But Toby had already guessed. What else could cause Hasan so much pain?

"It's Little Butterpat, isn't it? She was crying! But why? I thought the three of you were supposed to be so happy!"

A hunted look came over Hasan's face. He waved his hands about vaguely.

"No one is happy all the time. Even the heart may have a summer and a winter."

But Toby wasn't satisfied with that.

"Did the sultan stop loving her? Was that it?"

It seemed to Toby that Hasan was torn between saying nothing and defending his old friend. In the end, loyalty won.

"No, no. He loved her always. But as the years passed, he let himself care about his treasures more and more. 'Come and walk with me,' she would say to him. And he would reply: 'Soon, soon.' 'Come and talk to me.' 'Soon, soon.' And Little Butterpat would wander through the

palace, lonely and bored, while the sultan spent his time with his riches."

Without thinking, Toby burst out:

"You should have warned him! You should have given him a word of advice!"

Then he saw Hasan's face, and remembered. Hasan buried his head in his hands.

"I was a fool!" he cried. "I should have spoken!

40

What did it matter that I would lose everything and find myself outside the palace gates again, dusty and hungry! A man has no more goods than he gets good by. And the love of Little Butterpat – because it was a thing that could neither be bought nor sold – was worth more than all the treasures in the palace!"

Toby tried to comfort him.

"But the sultan was to blame too!"

Hasan lifted his head from his hands.

"Oh, yes. Blame the sultan too! For Little Butterpat came to the door of the counting house a thousand times. 'Come and dance with me.' 'Come and sing with me.' But the sultan only answered: 'Soon, soon.' And I – I cared more for all I had gained than for all I would lose, and said nothing – nothing at all!"

Hasan broke off, sobbing himself now.

Ping! Ping! Ping! Ping!

The golden tears rained down.

Hoping to comfort him, Toby moved closer and slipped an arm round his shoulder. To his astonishment, it felt brittle to his touch, and he couldn't help stepping back, startled.

Hasan lifted a face with gold tears rolling down but not a tearstain in sight.

Ping! Ping! Ping! Ping!

"See!" he cried. "Even my golden tears mock me! If Little Butterpat could only see the curse she put on me, her tears would flow as freely as mine do now!"

Ping! Ping! Ping! Ping!

Toby was horrified.

"She put a *curse* on you? What? Out of *spite*?"

The genie shook his head. Tears scattered far and wide.

Ping! Ping! Ping! Ping!

Taking a deep breath, Toby slid his arm around the genie's shoulders, and squeezed him as hard as he dare. Gradually, the pinging slowed.

Ping! Ping!

"Tell me what happened. Please. Finish the story."

Ping!

Kicking his last tear away, Hasan took up his tale.

CHAPTER FIVE

"Some days," said Hasan, "winds cut across the desert like hot knives. Dogs snapped and babies cried. Everyone stood at the door of ill-temper. And on one of those days, Zubaida came here, to the counting house."

Hasan stepped inside. Toby followed. Hasan pointed to some coin sacks in the corner.

"We had just counted those. The sultan was sitting watching us fill yet another sack, when in she walked."

"Come and dance with me!" murmured Toby. "Come and sing with me!"

The genie smiled. "And the sultan replied:

'Soon, soon.'"

"Everything the same as usual," said Toby.

"Not quite. For the hot winds had caught at Little Butterpat and sharpened her temper and nerves. 'Who could need all this gold?' she demanded of the sultan. 'All is not gain that is put in the purse. Your treasures are bought too dear. You have become a slave to your possessions. Even the richest man can carry nothing but his shroud away with him. So give your riches to those who will use them. He who learns giving as well as getting has no need for a counting house at all!'

"Then she turned and held her hands out to me.

"'Tell him, grand vizier!' she begged me."

Toby bit his lip. He could see that the genie was still ashamed of the memory.

"And I said nothing – not a word of advice."

"What happened?"

Hasan sighed. "Oh, it was not a day for lovers! The sultan was piqued. 'What do you know about these things?' he asked Little Butterpat scornfully. 'You who would spend your days dancing and talking, laughing and singing! What do you know about the value of things that can be bought and sold?'

"Now her eyes flashed.

"'More than you think,' she told him haughtily. 'I know the value of all the riches in this counting house!'

"The sultan's voice took on the edge of steel.

"'What's this?' he said. 'Can you see through the weave of a sack, and count the coins inside?' And he reached down to where, at his feet, lay a lamp so dull and rusty that no one had bothered

to lift it from the floor. Holding it high, he cried out to all who would listen:

"'Here is a prize for Little Butterpat, if she can tell me the value of all the riches in my counting house!'"

Toby felt his stomach knotting.

"It was a day fit only for dogs," said Hasan. "Drawing herself up, Zubaida replied with all the scorn of one who has spent too many days wandering alone through a palace:

"'Your riches are worth nothing!'"

Now Toby could see the sultan in Hasan's face, and hear him in his voice.

"'Nothing?'"

"'Nothing!'"

"'How so, my beloved?' he asked, dangerous as a cobra.

"'Because,' she cried, 'your riches are like camel dung! No use to anyone till they are spread!'

"'Camel dung!' shouted the sultan. Oh, it was a day for scorpions! And in his fury, he flung the lamp."

"Did it hit her?"

"It tangled in the folds of her robes. And as she reached to shake it off with one hand, she pointed at the sultan with the other.

"'Gold! Gold!' she cried. 'I wish you were turned to gold. And since you love gold more than the living, I wish I were turned to gold too!' Her fingers brushed the lamp, which suddenly started to glow. 'Stop!' cried the sultan. 'It is a magic lamp. Take back your wish, and quickly!' But she did not hear because in her anger she had turned to me.

"'As for you, grand vizier, I wish you were

imprisoned forever in this old lamp, cursed with a body turning day by day to gold, and forced to serve one greedy, grasping master after another until –'"

Hasan broke off.

"Until *what*?" Toby demanded. "Until *what*?"

Hasan shook his head.

"I may not say. And barely were the words out of her mouth before she was turned to gold, and the sultan too, and I – "

But Toby had shut his eyes and clapped his hands over his ears.

"Don't tell me any more! I can't stand it! It's too awful. Oh, how I wish the three of you could go back in time and start that day again!"

Now there it was, for the third time, that sudden catch of breath. Toby opened his eyes. Hasan was staring at him with a wild look of hope.

"Is that your third and last wish?"

Last? Oh, no! Only three wishes! He'd spent the first on a dish of sherbet, the second on a song, and now the third was going! How could things have worked out this way? But, then again, thought Toby. What would he wish for if he had more time to think? Only more stuff to clutter up his bedroom. And if he had learned anything at all from Hasan, it was that the things that could not be bought or sold were more valuable than anything else.

So let the wish go if it made Hasan happy.

"Yes! Yes! It's my third and last wish!"

The sudden glow of gold that lit the counting house was richer than any before. The air filled with soft scents and the glorious ripple of bird-song. And Hasan stood, taller than before, repeating softly under his breath the last words of Zubaida's wish.

" – cursed to serve one greedy, grasping master after another until you find one whose wishes are all for another, not for himself."

Now it was Toby's turn to stare.

"I've done it! Haven't I?"

The genie pressed his hands together, and bowed low.

"I had no hopes," he said. "I saw your room, crammed full of everything you ever owned, and my heart sank. But you have done it."

He had, too. Already shreds of gold were falling from Hasan, showering to the floor. His fingernails were peeling. The harsh gold of his eyes was changing back to soft brown, and from them tears were spilling onto the stones.

49

Splash! Splash! Splash! Splash!

Real tears! Hasan was weeping tears of joy, for before his very eyes the two golden statues were coming back to life, reaching for one another and smiling. The dreadful, dreadful day was starting all over again, but this time it would be different, and so would the future.

Then suddenly Hasan came to his senses.

"Quick!" he cried, brushing away his tears. "Hurry, before the glow fades and you are stuck forever out of time!"

Unfurling the carpet, he pushed Toby down flat.

"Shut your eyes! Hold tightly!"

He gave Toby no choice. Before the glow of gold could fade away entirely, the carpet rose. Rippling steadily, it flew up – up, up – high in the sky and away, and once again Toby could feel cool breezes lifting his hair.

He lay flat, as he'd been told, holding on tightly. Beneath him the carpet was soft. Indeed, the further it flew, the softer it felt, more like a duvet lulling Toby into drowsiness. When he got home again, he'd clear out his cupboards, give a lot of things away. What was the point of hanging on to everything? He didn't want to be a slave to his possessions. After all, even the richest man can carry nothing but his shroud away with him. And riches were only like camel dung really - not much use till they were spread.

He'd take the games and models and some of the other stuff he hardly ever used down to the charity shop on the corner. And he could give Sophie the comics. As soon as he got home he'd stack the whole lot in boxes and carry them out of his room.

That way Mum would get to see her dear son's face again . . .

That would be good . . .

Before the journey even ended, Toby was asleep.